Won't You Be My KISSAROO?

JOANNE RYDER   MELISSA SWEET

www.hmhbooks.com

Library of Congress Cataloging-in-Publication Control Number 2002014581
ISBN 978-0-547-32792-1

Printed in China
LEO 10 9 8 7 6 5 4 3 2 1
4500248092

To Larry, my dear kissaroo
—J.R.
To Henry
—M.S.

Won't you be my *kissaroo*?
I've lots of kisses just for you.

A morning kiss is full of sun
and wishes for the day to come.

A breakfast kiss is nice and sweet.
It's fun when sticky lips can meet.

A good-bye kiss goes with a hug
to keep you safe and feeling snug.

A hello kiss is soft as rain.
It's good to see your face again.

A puppy kiss is very wet,
as silly as a kiss can get.

A kitten kiss is just a lick,
a friendly touch, so light and quick.

A playful kiss will often squeak
and make a **Pop!** upon your cheek.

A gotcha kiss surprises you
with tickles and some giggles, too.

A birthday kiss, while candles glow,
will make you **grow**

and **grow**

and **grow**.

A bedtime kiss will tuck you tight
and keep you cozy through the night.

So . . .
Won't you be my kissaroo?
And every day, the whole day through,
we'll share *new* kisses . . .

. . . me and you!